THE ADVENTURES OF

JULIA

THE GENEROSITY GENIE

A middle-grade novel by

DEBORAH BLOHM

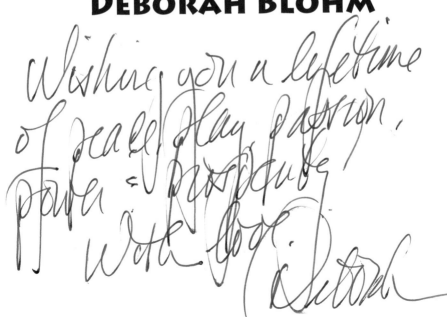

Wishing you a lifetime
of peace, play passion,
power & purpose.
With love,
Deborah

This Book is Dedicated to:

My beautiful, wide-eyed daughter, Sofia.

May your life be one wonder-filled, blessed and sacred adventure after another....

You are my greatest blessing and joy!

And to my amazing nephews, Cameron and Harrison.

You always happily impress and astound me!

To my loving, supportive sisters, Nicole & Kristina.

You are brilliant and beautiful.

And thank you, Mom & Dad, Lina and Ted for instilling strong, healthy values and a "you can do anything/never give up" attitude.

I cannot imagine my life without any of you.

I love you.

The Adventures of Julia the Generosity Genie
© 2011 Deborah Blohm
Published by: DB Designs, Inc.
ISBN: 978-0-615-57002-0
Library of Congress Catalogue No. 2011944504

Suggested reading level: middle grades, ages 8–12
To contact the author, please email:
Deborah Blohm
deborah@generositygenie.com

Book Design: Bill Walker
(www.billwalkerdesigns.com)

Cover Design & Interior Illustrations: Simon Scales
(www.simonscales.com.au)

First Edition
1 3 5 7 9 10 8 6 4 2

Manufactured by Thomson-Shore, Dexter, MI (USA); RMA578TB859, December 2011

Join our 2012 Treasure Hunt Adventure

Julia, The Generosity Genie and all of her Friends ~ most importantly You!
Hunt for the hidden **Green Jade Mask**
Place: The United States of America

Beginning January 21, 2012

Ending December 21, 2012

Please email: **deborah@generositygenie.com** with your name, email address, city, state and age.

Friend us on Facebook Fan Page
Julia the Generosity Genie, follow us on Twitter **JuliaGenGGirl** and **www.generositygenie.com** for Clue postings as well.

You will receive your First Clue by email January 21st

Every month on the 21st you will receive a Clue.

November 21st find the final Clue and the *Green Jade Mask.*

The Winners will be announced on December 21, 2012.

The Top 3 Winners will receive a **Chest filled with Treasures.**

TABLE OF CONTENTS

THE STORM

The fierce storm came out of nowhere, catching Julia, William, Cool Cat, and Loria off guard. They quickly put on their bright yellow rain jackets and began their journey back from the jungle. Suddenly, Julia lost her balance. Before she could right herself, she was tumbling down a dark hole hidden in the ground. She hit the bottom with a loud splash. Julia's heart pounded as she anxiously treaded water and screamed into the darkness for help.

Silently, Loria, Julia's pet butterfly whispered, "Be still; find your inner peace; you will be fine no matter what happens. Remember your power gems and the colors...."

William, Julia's little brother, felt his entire body shake as he looked down the seemingly bottomless

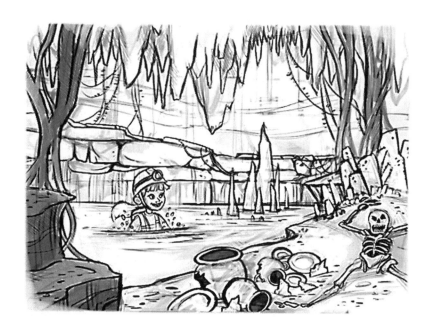

black pit. Frantically, he grabbed his flashlight from his well-stocked tool belt hanging low across his hips and shined it on Julia's muddy brown face.

"Julia!" William exclaimed as he held tightly onto the nearby ceiba tree with one hand. "Are you all right? Are you hurt?" The violent winds and pounding rain were pushing William and Cool Cat, Julia's pet cat, back and forth in the tropical landscape.

Julia, treading water, quickly took off her yellow jacket and said, "I think I'm all right. I twisted my ankle when I fell. It hurts, but I think I'm okay." She touched her colorful bejeweled pendant. Her fingers specifically sought out its red and purple gemstones; when she thought she found them she imagined the power colors red and purple filling her with courage, strength, and protection.

"Can you see anything?" William asked.

"No, it's completely dark, and the water is cold! Can you tie a vine around your hardhat—you know, the one with the attached flashlight?—and lower it down to me?"

William quickly searched for a long vine, took off his favorite red hardhat that was fully equipped with a powerful light, extra batteries, and a few hidden tools, carefully tied them all together, and lowered it about 20 feet down to where Julia was splashing about and trying not to go under the chilly water.

The hardhat lit up the whole sinkhole or *cenote*, in Spanish. Julia was surprised to see that the *cenote* was spectacular: a few bats awoke in the beam of light and began to fly about the enormous cave; large stalactites hung from the ceiling; and the stalagmites protruded from the ground—making it look like crystals glittered from ceiling to floor. One area shone more brightly; it seemed to have a single crystal formation, and it sparkled like a trillion diamonds.

Julia was stunned. For a moment she forgot she was stuck deep in a hole and soaked in very cold water. She noticed an area of dry ground, quickly swam over, and surveyed her surroundings.

A few large crayfish and spiders scurried away, making her notice that there were lots of pieces of pottery scattered about. She also took note of a trail of rocks leading up to the sparkling crystal formation. Strangely, she thought smelled roasted corn and flour tortillas! Was she just starving? Or had she lost her marbles? That was when she noticed the pulsing throb in her ankle. She bent down to examine it.

"William!" Julia exclaimed. "I'm on dry ground! And my ankle is worse than I thought. It's really badly sprained."

"Julia," William stated, "attached inside my hardhat is gauze and a bandage to wrap up your ankle."

"Wow, William! You always amaze me!" Julia replied. "Thank goodness you're always prepared! Thanks!" Happy to be out of the cold water but shivering from her soaking clothing, Julia wrapped her ankle tightly and found a walking stick to help her hobble around. The air inside the hole was hot and humid. Julia, careful not to place pressure on her ankle, ascended a stone staircase toward the sparkling crystal formation. The entire cave was mesmerizing—a grand holy place.

William called down. "What do you see?" His voice bounced off the cave walls, echoing: "...see... see...see...?"

"I found a nativity scene made of crystal! It looks like a room, too small to walk into, filled with 10 to 50 inches of stalagmite and stalactite crystal formations. It looks like it came right out of our favorite gem book, you know, the one called *Gemstones*. You know that all of these quartz crystals attract powerful life force energy. I can even see that some of the crystals are clear and others are purple, yellow, and light brown."

"I think, from what I've learned, that ancient people once worshiped their gods in cave holes like this one. This must have been a cathedral." She continued to survey the cave, noticing, but not touching, broken pottery, a mortar and pestle, and various stoneware and other unrecognizable objects. She noticed that some of the cave formations had been modified: One was shaped like an altar for ceremonial offerings, and the silhouettes of others might have been made to look like human and animal faces and bodies. The cave, in Spanish called an *actún*, was truly magnificent looking at all the treasures it revealed under the light of the hardhat.

William called out, "Julia! We're going to need help getting you out of there. This storm is terrible—and getting worse. Cool Cat will stay here by the opening while I go find help." William ran back toward town and disappeared into the darkness.

Cool Cat, Julia's language translating pet, was terrified. He shivered and stated in Spanish, "¿Estas bien?...Are you all right? ¿Que ves? What do you see? Mercielagos...bats, cangrejos de rio grandes...large crayfish, arañas...spiders!"

Julia nodded as if the feline could see her and continued to walk throughout the enormous cave. In the back left corner she found a simpler staircase leading to another smaller cave. Carefully and slowly, so as not to hurt her ankle even more, she climbed up and entered the small room. "Agh!" she cried as she stumbled. Upon closer examination of the object on the floor, she saw the remains of a human skeleton positioned as if seated in the corner. Her eyes widened.

Meanwhile, up above the ground, William ran down the slippery, muddy path, tripped, and fell over what turned out to be a Mayan boy about his age. "I'm sorry!" he exclaimed. "Are you all right?"

Three other boys stood close by and started pointing and laughing and yelling, "Cross-eyed freak! Flathead!"

William caught his breath. Who had he fallen over? The other boys ran off in the rain.

The Mayan boy looked relieved. "Wow, you surprised me! Thanks for scaring off those boys! But this heavy storm swept my dog's house—his name is Rao—out to sea. Oh yeah, and I'm Juan."

"I'm William." The two boys fist-bumped. "Who were those boys? Why are they calling you names?" William asked, noticing that the boy indeed had crossed eyes, and his face *was* sort of flat looking.

"Their names are Tarke, Clark, and Marque," Juan replied in a low voice. He was clearly afraid of them. "They're three older boys who like to make fun of me because I'm different from them: My eyes are crossed and my forehead is flatter than most people's."

"They're just bullies," William responded. "Bullies like to gang up on people. I'm happy to stand up for you and help rebuild your doghouse tomorrow, but today we have to save my sister. She's fallen into a hidden *cenote*. Will you help us?"

"Absolutely!" said Juan. "Let's grab some rope and go! She must have fallen into the sacred cave,

Actún Tunichil Muknal." They ran off and Juan's dog, Rao, followed. The storm's vicious wind blew fiercely as they fought to get back to Julia.

Still deep inside the *cenote*, Julia was busy exploring, something she always did wherever she went—even with a sprained ankle. She was examining the skeleton. It looked small, as if it had been a child's body once upon a time. She took a closer look at the bones but could not see any breaks or cracks. So if the child had not been hurt and died, then maybe he or she, deduced Julia, had been sacrificed in some form of ancient ritual.

Aboveground, William and Juan reached the one of the *cenote*'s openings. Working together, they lowered the rope to Julia. She heard the echo of their voices saying, "Grab on, Julia!", secured the rope to her waist, and held on as, slowly and carefully, the two boys pulled her to safety.

Relieved, Cool Cat sighed, "*Me llamo Juan...* my name is Juan. *¿Podrias tu ayudarnos a rescatar a ella?...*Will you help rescue her? *Trabajando juntos...* working together. *La fuerza del gema y el color rojo para coraje...*the power of the gem and the color red for courage. *La fuerza del gema y el color morado para protección...*the power of the gem and the color purple for protection."

THE DISCOVERY

The next morning, the sun shone brightly, as though yesterday's terrible storm had never happened. Julia, William, and their animal friends had been in Belize for the last week to help their mother research the medicinal value of the local flora and fauna. Julia and William had left early for Julia's doctor's appointment to check her sprained ankle.

They walked a path that was surrounded by young spiky kapok, or *ceiba*, trees, bamboo, and a peculiar-looking green leafy plant. Following closely behind were Julia's three favorite pets: Cool Cat, Unity, and Loria. Cool Cat, Julia's fluffy white Himalayan fur-ball of a cat, leisurely followed along, mumbling. He always mumbled in the native language, and on this trip to South America, he was mumbling in the native

17

Spanish language: "*Pasado del parque*...past the park."

Unity, her beautiful white dove, flew peacefully from branch to branch as Loria, Julia's colorful pet butterfly—deep vivid blues, purples, and yellows fluttered in the warm breeze. The local macaws were loudly squawking, the green poisonous dart frogs croaked menacingly, and a few red dragonflies danced about the windblown, tropical landscape.

Julia loved all animals, but most of all her beloved three pets. Cool Cat was a genius with languages; he was fluent in every single one and was forever translating words and phrases for everyone around him. He couldn't help himself. Unity radiated grace as she soared, spreading peace throughout the land. And Loria provided Julia with daily guidance and loving support. Loria, Unity, and Cool Cat followed Julia and William everywhere. They were their special support team and advisors—and they always did their best to keep William and Julia safe and out of harm's way.

Julia and William felt at home exploring the world and helping others, yet they had no way of knowing that this journey would be a journey like none other. It would change their lives forever.

Returning home from the doctor's office, the group

ran into Juan; Rao was happily digging in the dirt. In the bright sunlight, they could better see that Juan had a seemingly flatter-than-normal forehead, and his eyes were definitely crossed. He *was* different; but Julia and William could have cared less. He was nice and friendly and so was his dog.

Julia said, "Hello, Juan! How are you? What a nice surprise running into you. Thank you for helping me out of the *cenote* yesterday!"

Juan replied, "You're welcome. How is your ankle?" Rao, having tired himself out and now resting peacefully, barely opened one eye to see who was speaking. His wet nose was covered in dirt.

Cool Cat smiled lazily. "*Hola!*...Hello. *¿Como estas?*...How are you? *Ese perro esta cansadissimo...* that dog is super sleepy."

"We were just at the doctor's office. She said my ankle has a minor sprain and should heal pretty quickly," responded Julia as she imagined the power color green soothingly healing her ankle.

Juan replied, "Great news! You were lucky; you really fell a long way down!"

Julia responded, "Yes, lucky and very blessed. We must have a million angels watching over us. What an interesting cave, it smelled of corn and tortillas and was filled with beautiful gems and crystals. I even found a human skeleton!"

"Yes, you stumbled into a sacred *actún* that was used in ancient Mayan rituals. My brother Pedro would know more about the ceremonies performed in the caves," said Juan.

"I look forward to learning more when we talk to Pedro. Can we meet him today?"

"Yes, Pedro would love to meet you. But first, would you please help me rebuild Rao's doghouse so he has a nice place to sleep tonight after yesterday's storm?"

"I'm happy you asked! Rao looks wiped out. Sure, I can help. I have tools; and I'm a very good builder!" William proudly showed off his overloaded tool belt complete with hammers, saws, drills, nails, measuring tools, tape, and almost anything else one could imagine. His greatest joy was building.

"Thank you," Juan said gratefully. "I'm looking for the strongest pieces of bamboo to start with."

Cool Cat replied, "*Me encantaría ayudar*...I would love to help. *Muy bueno*...very good. *Si, perfecto!*...yes, perfect! *Gracias*...thank you!" It was as if Cool Cat was letting them all know that Spanish was a relatively simple language—and a good one to know!

They all began separating the bamboo, stacking the stronger pieces to their right and the weaker pieces to their left.

Cool Cat nodded, "*Si, a la derecha*...to the right; *a la izquierda*...to the left." Busily they worked: stringing and tying, cutting and fastening, knot after knot. Hours later the strong, new, bamboo doghouse was nearly complete.

Loria the butterfly whispered to Julia, "Great work! You've been so generous and very helpful today!"

They carefully moved the doghouse close to the

exact western-facing spot where Rao would sleep. Julia suggested they dig deep into the earth to create a secure foundation for the doghouse. As they dug, Julia excitedly pointed to a small dark green slab peeking through the dirt. "Something is there. It looks like a medallion of some kind!"

Juan picked it up, "Wow! Look at this!" Stunned, he held up a carved jade medallion and handed it to Julia.

She examined it closely. "It looks like an ancient jade medallion that someone once wore as a piece of jewelry— even the string is still attached. The front carving looks to be Jacmul, the elusive black jaguar revered by all Mayans. And it has a very interesting carving on the back...some kind of map?" Julia had studied a lot about Mayan culture and knew all sorts of interesting facts about ancient Mayan history and artifacts.

"Maybe it is an ancient treasure map!" William exclaimed.

Julia responded, musingly. "Highly possible. I think we may have found something very special that requires further investigation as soon as we're done here." Julia carefully placed the medallion in her pocket as the three finished securing the final pieces of Rao's new doghouse.

Juan thanked everyone. "I couldn't have done this without you! You've helped me so much *and* made it fun. Now we've found this ancient medallion, and now my curiosity is nearly killing me! I can't wait to begin our adventure!"

Suddenly, to their dismay, Tarke, Clark, and Marque—the bullies who had been bothering Juan—ran by, laughed, and yelled, "Hey, crosseyed, flathead freak, bet another storm'll totally wreck your dumb doghouse."

"Stop it! Get lost!" Julia yelled, instinctively picturing the power gem citrine and the color yellow for personal power and confidence.

As the boys ran off, William asked, "What's wrong with those boys?"

"I wish I knew," Juan replied sadly. "I've never done anything to them. They just don't like me because I'm not like they are. It makes me feel bad."

Julia put her hand on Juan's arm and said, "Juan, I used to be bullied, too. It really hurts. Then I learned how to stand up for myself. I learned that bullies have often been bullied or abused themselves, and they just want power or control over someone else to get some relief from their own feelings of powerlessness."

"I didn't know bullies felt powerless! Just knowing that gives me a new feeling of confidence."

"Yes, they intimidate others to cover up their own insecurities and inadequacies," Julia continued. "They take their anger and their own hurt out on others—especially those whom they perceive to be vulnerable. I would be happy to share with you what I did to fend off the bullies who were making my life miserable."

Juan perked up. "Please tell me. I want to learn how to be powerful and better stand up for myself—and for others who might need help!"

Julia responded, "I call it the Four Ss: Safety first, Stick together, Speak up, and Support those being bullied. The first priority is your own safety; you always have to protect yourself. Walk away if you can, and act like you don't care, even if you really do. Sometimes you can't walk away, so you have to protect yourself so you can *then* get away or run away. And try not to let them get to you. If you walk away or ignore them, they won't get the satisfaction they're looking for. Also, I use power gems and colors to help me access feelings such as strength, courage, self-confidence, and protection. The power gems amethyst and color purple is used to access feelings of insight and protection, I imagine myself throwing off an intense vibrant purple light."

William chimed in, "Second, stick together, stay in a group. Get others involved whenever you're dealing with bullies. Remember: Bullies like to pick on people who are alone. Find opportunities to make new friends. Explore your interests, join in school or community activities, volunteer, and participate in community service."

Julia continued, "William is right on. Third, speak up against the bully; look the bully in the eye and say: 'Stop it!' To help me feel confident, I picture the power color bright yellow and the power color deep red for courage. Don't be afraid to get help, and whatever you do, don't be ashamed or blame yourself. No matter what they say, there are wonderful things about you. Keep those in mind instead of the disrespectful messages you get from the people who are bullying you. Be proud of who you are, and be sure not to bully back. Speak up, and let the adults, teachers, parents or even your school counselors know about the bullying. Talk to someone you trust; teachers, counselors, and others are there to help."

William piped up with, "And finally, support and stand up for others who are being bullied. We all have to stand up to the bullies and intervene when someone needs help. Lots of times adults and others must be involved for the bullying to stop. You can't always do it alone."

"Very true, William. Keep doing what you love to do and you will defeat the bully," Julia added.

Juan repeated, "Wow! The Four Ss: Safety first, Stick together, Speak up, and Support others.... Thank you. I'll do my best next time to stand up for myself and stop the bullying!" As he walked off, Juan imagined himself giving off the power of the power gems and the colors deep red for courage and purple for protection; that would help him for sure. And in his mind's eye he pictured himself speaking up to the bullies with his supportive friends surrounding him—and Tarke, Clark and Marque running off, never to bully him again.

Cool Cat proudly stated, "*Las cuatro Ss:* the Four S's. *Primero asegurate:* Safety first. *Estar pegados...* Stick together. *Dilo!*...Speak up! *Apoya estos siendo peleadores...*Support those being bullied. *Se orgulloso de quien eres...*be proud of who you are. *Promover la paz para sentirse vivo...*promote peace-filled lives." She smiled and began to imagine herself throwing off the power gem amethyst and the color purple for protection. "*La fuerza del color morado para proteccion...* the power of the color purple for protection. *La fuerza del color amarillo para la confianza...*the power of the color yellow for confidence."

All of them, especially Rao in his cozy new doghouse, had a sound night's sleep before the next day's journey. Their minds raced in wonder about where this ancient jade medallion might take them. No one could imagine what possibilities lay ahead.

Julia affectionately turned to Cool Cat. "My worldly word kitty, where will this adventure lead us?"

As she drifted off to sleep, Cool Cat purred, "*Si, la espera de las maravillas*...the wonders await. *Que posibilidades hay en el futuro!*...What possibilities lie ahead! *Descanses bien*...rest well, *mañana será un día ajetreado*...tomorrow will be a busy day. *Buenas noches*...good night."

Unity gracefully landed in her nest, wondering if all would go smoothly. Loria perched herself on a lily as her fluttering wings came to a halt; she knew something powerful and life changing was about to happen to all of them.

POWERFUL JADE

Julia awoke early, greeting the morning sun's golden rays while performing her sun salutation yoga moves that she liked to do every morning upon awakening. Cool Cat was stretched out by her side. Unity watched from a branch of an old plum tree, and Loria fluttered about, landing on flowers here and there.

William and Juan awoke and excitedly ran to join Julia. Rao followed, barking loudly as he had a great night's sleep in his new doghouse. Julia greeted them, pulling out the rare jade medallion. They intently studied what indeed looked like a map. What did it lead to?

The map carvings had what looked like an oval-shaped island with three fingers jutting out. On the middle finger, seven trees gradually decreased in size, with a large X marking a spot. Another deeply etched

X, this one enclosed within a big circle, was marked in what seemed to be smack in the middle of the ocean.

Julia asked, "Juan, does this map look familiar? Something that looks like an island with three protruding fingers?"

Juan replied, "*Sí!* Yes, I've heard about the three-fingered Half Moon Cay Island. My mother once told me a story about a mystical island with three fingers covered with large seashells. Legend says it is covered in gemstones!"

William exclaimed, "Wow, an island covered in gemstones! I wonder what kind of gems?"

"Maybe sapphires, rubies, emeralds, or jade! I

think it'll most likely be jade. Jade has been found and revered here for thousands of years!" Julia cried. Julia and William's family going way back had shared a passion and a quest for knowledge about gemstones for centuries.

Cool Cat smiled and began counting from zero to ten in Spanish: "*Cero, uno, dos, tres, cuatro, cinco, seis, siete, ocho, nueve, diez*...0, 1, 2, 3, 4, 5, 6, 7, 8, 9, 10. *Tres dedos*...Three fingers, *siete árboles*...seven trees, *X marca el terreno*...X marks the spot, *piedra preciosa*... precious gems, *mucho jade*...lots of jade."

Julia heard Loria, her pet butterfly state, "Step back!" Julia did so immediately just as a huge black crow swooped down, barely missing her head.

"Gosh!" exclaimed Juan. "I've never seen a crow do that!"

Julia nodded. "No kidding! I guess we always have to remain aware. He could have been trying to scare us and steal the jade medallion or something else!" Unity, the dove, followed the black crow to figure out who or what wanted to upset the peace. Maybe someone had sent their pet to scare them all away somehow.

Julia continued. "For the ancient Mayans, jade symbolized life, fertility, eternity, and power. It was treasured beyond any other material, only to be worn and used by the nobility. They wore great quantities of jade beads wrapped around their necks and waists and placed in pockets, and they even inlaid jade in their teeth! Jade was also made into weapons and tools because it is a hard and tough gemstone."

"Wow, Jade sounds beautiful, powerful, painful, *and* useful. I'd like to make all of my tools out of jade!"

Julia laughed. "William, what a great idea: learning the art of gem carving! You know, the Mayans considered jade their most precious possession—more precious than gold!—and believed it even had medicinal powers to help cure lung and kidney ailments. The power gem jade and the color green is used to help heal our bodies."

Julia continued. She was on a roll. "Jade comes in lots of colors, actually. The Mayans prized the colors of apple and emerald green. Jadeite is white in its pure state, with the other colors caused by inclusions of other minerals. For example, it is the mineral chromium that gives jadeite its vibrant green color and manganese that gives jade a lilac color. In Guatemala, which is next to Belize, you can find lots of jadeite in natural colors of lilac, blue, pink, white, yellow, and black. There's also a unique black jade with natural precious metals such as gold, silver, and platinum speckled throughout the gem. Guatemala is now producing the world's newest jadeite colors, including 'rainbow Jadeite,' which is several colors all in one."

Juan remarked, "My favorite color is blue. I remember seeing one of the Grand Council members wearing a simple, carved, blue jade figure of a person around her neck; I was practically mesmerized."

"Oh yes, blue jade is very special and rare; it was used by the Olmec people many years before the Maya used it. The Olmec were master jade artisans who perfected carving human figures out of precious stones. Blue jade is only found in one place in the world, Motagua Valley, a river valley in Guatemala. The power color blue is used for prosperity and peaceful communication," Julia responded.

"Didn't Grandpa Wally once tell us that jadeite is hard, dense, and scarce, and that it's formed under enormous pressures at low temperatures in the earth? And didn't he say that it sells for hundreds to thousands of dollars a carat?"

"I can't believe you remembered that, William! Jade was one of Grandfather's favorite gemstones!"

Cool Cat wondered what made colors so powerful in the first place; it must be its vibrating energy. *"La fuerza del color verde para curarse o sanarse...*the power color green for curing and healing. *La fuerza del color azul para la prosperidad y la* comunicación pacífica... the power color blue for prosperity and peaceful communication."

Juan was very excited. "We have to find Pedro! He knows so much about our people, land, and history. We have to show him this ancient jade medallion. He might even know if it's possible to get to Half Moon Cay Island!"

All three kids and all three of Julia's pets plus Juan's dog excitedly made for the boat docks to look for Pedro. They got lucky, for there he was, working on his speedboat.

THE QUEST

Pedro, who was a lot older than Julia, had known
Juan since he was a toddler, and for all practical
purposes, they were brothers. Just like in the biblical
story in which baby Moses was found in a basket
floating down the reed-filled waters of a river in the the
land of the Pharaoh, Juan had actually been spotted
by Pedro's mother floating down the Subin River in
a small basket. She immediately took him in as her
own. No one knew what had caused Juan's mother to
abandon him, but he certainly was beloved by his new
family.

Unknown to Juan, Julia, and William, they were
being followed by Dr. J. D. Diamond and the black
crow that had attacked Julia earlier. They were actually
very close behind the children, and they kept ducking

behind trees and buildings so the kids, if they had turned around by chance, would not catch them.

Dr. J. D. Diamond had once been a great friend and colleague of Julia and William's father, Theodore Leon. Theodore Leon and Dr. Diamond had met while studying gemstones at the prestigious Gemological Institute of America. Theodore had gone on to study the art of watch making, while Dr. Diamond began exploring the world for treasures with Theodore's father, Wally Leon, a world-renowned explorer and archeologist.

But Dr. Diamond was not a good guy. He focused only on himself, his own needs and wants. He did not share or help others. He even became so greedy that he began to steal. He was caught trying to take a priceless, precious gemstone from the Smithsonian Institute in Washington, DC. He quickly managed to get expelled from the Archeological Society because of his corrupt and controlling nature, and was actually banned from ever re-entering the United States.

Now his only friend was Crow, a sneaky and fidgety bird who shared his nasty reputation in the art of deception and thievery and kept him informed about whatever secrets he could find out that might help the Doctor. And Dr. Diamond would stop at nothing to get the magical pendant that Julia was wearing back into his possession. Dr. Diamond and Crow had been following them since they had arrived in South America. Very methodically, calculatingly, and menacingly they watched the group. Unity, the dove, soon realized that Crow was with Dr. Diamond—and knew Julia and William had to be warned.

Back at the boat docks, Pedro studied the Jade medallion carefully and slowly asked, "Where...did you...find this?"

"We found it while we were building a new doghouse for Rao. It was buried in the dirt next to the Ceiba trees and bamboo fields right by Rao's old doghouse," answered Juan.

Pedro nodded. "Hmmm, legends say that an old tribal medicine doctor hid a special mystical green jade mask, to be found one day only by a very special person who will lead our country and bring peace to our people. This is supposed to be a legend, but this medallion is *authentic*! And yes, I know where this three-fingered island is, and I'm very interested in the X circled in the middle of the ocean. I have a feeling this is the difficult-to-get-to Blue Hole."

Julia frowned, puzzled. "What's the Blue Hole?"

"The Blue Hole is an underwater coral formation about a three and a half hour boat ride away. Interestingly, the coral reef formed in the middle of the ocean in a circular pattern, which can only be seen when you're high in the sky looking down on the area. But when you're there, you only see the deep blue water and no land. Apparently, when you dive deep into the Blue Hole, there are old caves with huge 40-foot stalactites hanging from the ceilings," Pedro said.

"Wow! More quartz crystals attracting powerful life force energy!" Julia blurted.

"Pedro, have you ever been to the Blue Hole?" asked William.

"No, but it looks like today may be the day we visit the Half Moon Cay Island *and* the Blue Hole. Let's prepare plenty of drinking water, food, and our diving equipment. If I understand this medallion's map correctly, we just *may* find a clue in the caves at the Blue Hole!"

Cool Cat murmured, "*¿Donde?*...Where? *Hasta la carreterra*...up the road. *Dispuesto a ir* ...ready to go! *Los cristales de cuarzo atraen la fuerza y la energia de la vida*...quartz crystals attract life force energy. *Manos a la obre*...let's get to work."

William and Juan gave each other a big fist bump and hurried off to make beans and corn tortillas for their journey. Juan showed William how to boil the corn kernels with white lime and water. And then grind it with a mortar and pestle to make the best fresh homemade tortillas. Julia prepared the diving equipment.

Cool Cat smiled and said in Spanish, "*Agujero azul*...blue hole; *cuevas viejos*...old caves; *techo*...ceiling; *agua potable*...drinking water; *maize*...corn; *tortillas*...tortillas."

THE CIRCLE OF Ps

As they all worked to get ready for their journey to the island and the Blue Hole, Pedro noticed the pendant Julia was wearing. "Your pendant is unusual. I've never seen anything like it."

Julia began to explain the long search for the missing triangular centerpiece, the fight between the Diamond family and the Leon family—her family— for ownership of this very pendant, and the magical powers it holds once the triangle is set into its center. "My dream is to find this missing piece one day while I'm still alive to see what it can do!"

Pedro examined the pendant. "Yes, I see the triangular space. What do the Circle of Ps and the colorful gemstones that surround the triangle mean?"

Julia proudly touched her pendant, then

responded, "My grandfather Wally gave it to me; it was passed down from his great grandfather...and he shared with me the special meanings of the Circle of Ps. As the story goes, the first P represents Peace: the beauty of peace throughout the world. Every living being, animal, insect, plant, and human will one day live in peace.

We deserve to live a peace-filled life. The power gem and the color for peace is blue." Upon hearing this, Unity the dove fluttered joyfully. "The second P represents Play: play being a very important part of daily living to keep us healthy and vibrant. Play with your friends, animals, imagination while learning and growing all the while. The power gem and the color for play is orange. The third P represents Passion: living from your heart, feeling happy, and enjoying whatever you are doing no matter—"

Julia was interrupted by William and Juan as they came bounding in with lunch bags of fresh tortillas and lots of fruit— oranges, mangos, and plums—the fruits of the Mayan kings.

William exclaimed, "We're all stocked up for our boat ride! I learned how to make beans with corn tortillas, bread nut, and another cross-eyed man gave us six ears of fresh grilled *maize* on the cob!" *Maize* is the Spanish name for corn.

Juan grinned. "I love *maize* on the cob!"

Pedro laughed. "Yes, *maize* just like our Mayan ancestors ate. They had a corn feast to celebrate before the blundering slaughter."

William and Juan looked puzzled. "Slaughter? Who said anything about a slaughter! We're just looking for treasure!"

A movement to his left caused Juan to flinch. Tarke, Clark, and Marque approach as they yelled, "Flathead, cross-eyed freak, flathead! . . ." Just then Juan felt an unusual feeling of strong confidence and the power color yellow well up inside of him. His hand raised, palm out, and he loudly shouted, "Stop it! Get lost!" It was an amusing coincidence that he had chosen to wear a bright yellow shirt that day.

Pedro, Julia, and William all chimed in. "Stop it! Get lost! We don't need you bullies around here!" The boys stopped in their tracks, looking stunned. Then, as if obeying some silent command, they turned around and ran away.

"Are those bullies still bothering you? I've had it with their behavior. I am letting Mother, your teacher, and the principal know today. Their bullying is totally unacceptable. They need to be stopped for good!" said Pedro forcefully.

"Thanks. I do feel stronger now that I know the tools for fending off bullies, but I still need your help and support to make it stick!" replied Juan.

Pedro, Julia, and William all nodded. "We're happy to help. Bullying is intolerable," added Julia. "Like I said: We all deserve to live peace-filled lives."

Pedro, who was as fascinated with the Mayan history as Julia, continued to talk about the Mayan culture. "The ancient Mayans believed that the blood of the gods mixed with *maize* created humans. They believed humans were birthed from the underworld and had to give back to the gods through human sacrifice and bloodletting. They strongly believed the underworld determined their prosperity, and they respected and adored their gods. Though no worries, blood sacrifice isn't practiced anymore by the modern Maya."

"The Mayans must have performed these rituals at the cave I stumbled into...Actún Tunichil Muknal."

"You fell into Actun Tunichil Muknal? That is one of the most sacred caves of the Mayans. It is highly revered. The Mayans still go into the cave to pray and ask for guidance even though there are no more sacrificial rituals being practiced."

"I totally felt the mystical energy surrounded by all the those gems and crystals. I understand their being drawn back to the sacred space."

Pedro said, "They did respect nature and all of its offerings! I feel blessed to be Mayan. And blessed to have met you, Julia, William, Cool Cat, Unity, and Loria! Treasure of our old Mayan king and the search for the magical green jade mask, here we come."

Excitedly they hopped into the small boat, Pedro at the helm, Julia sitting co-pilot with Loria perched on her shoulder, and William, Juan, and Cool Cat in the back. As he soared peacefully above the ocean waters, Unity let Julia know that Crow was with Dr. Diamond.

Cool Cat was hungry and could only think of fish. *"Pescado*...fish; *atún*...tuna; *delfín*...dolphin; *ballena*... whales; *ray picadura*...stingrays; *barracuda*; and *tiburónes*...sharks."* Barracuda! Sharks! Suddenly he was not so hungry anymore! The thought of being lunch for some toothy fish made him more than a little scared. Then realized how blessed he was amid all his friends and shouted, *"Nosotros sentimos bendecidos al conocerles*. . . We feel blessed to know you all!"*

THE BLUE HOLE

Pedro, Julia, William, Cool Cat, Unity, and Loria sped along, passing jumping spinner dolphins and frigate birds and spotting large manta rays in the clear, blue waters. They sped through small squalls of light rain showers as the sun glistened all around them, reflecting at times blindingly off the surface of the ocean. In the distance, they could see the oval-shaped island.

"There's Half Moon Cay Island. We have to be close to the famous Blue Hole. Let's get our scuba gear and prepare for the dive. The first part of the treasure map suggests we dive here. Maybe we'll find a clue in the cave!" Pedro shouted over the whirr of the boat motor.

Suited up, Julia leaned forward into a diving

position, saying excitedly, "Ready? Fire! Aim!" as she and Pedro dove into the cool ocean waters.

Pedro sputtered and laughed. "Isn't the saying: Ready? Aim! Fire?"

Julia smiled, trying not to dislodge her face mask. "Fire before aiming because we can always correct along the way, as long as we take action and go!"

Pedro smiled back. "Nice! I like the idea of taking action first and correcting our course as we go!"

William, Juan, Loria, Unity, and Cool Cat watched from the boat. Cool Cat purred, "*Vámanos*...let's go; *buena suerte*...good luck. *Hasta luego*...see you later."

As they descended into the depths of the ocean, they passed graceful sea fans, colorful sponges, and exquisite corals. A few small fish scurried about. They dove to 126 feet deep and soon caught sight of a large cave. Inside they could see the famed, enormous, 40-foot stalactites hanging from the ceiling.

Julia followed Pedro inside the cave. Pedro pointed at the strange and colorful drawing on one of the cave walls. It looked like a Mayan king wearing goggles around his eyes; he also sported a large headdress of Jacmul's face, the jaguar with red feathers, multiple strands of jade circled his neck, and he held a spear thrower in his left hand. Pedro recognized him as Fire

Is Born, the first notable Mayan king to rule this land in 378 ACE.

They noticed the green jade mask he held in his right hand and realized it must be the magical mask they were looking for! The mask was simple, refined yet striking; the face looked peaceful and serene. It had a large circle earring and a rectangular shaped headdress with a red triangular shaped object in its center. The mask radiated power and prosperity. The drawing also had an owl, a dove, an eagle, a frog, and a butterfly surrounding King Fire Is Born. Julia and Pedro wondered if these were the clues they were looking for that would lead to the treasure of Half Moon Cay.

As they ascended, they noticed a small school of Caribbean sharks circling in the distance—nothing to worry about for they were actually harmless. William and the rest anxiously awaited their return.

Julia popped out of the water first, followed by Pedro. Julia said, "What an amazing dive! The caves were magnificent, and I believe we have found the missing clues to help in the treasure hunt for the green jade mask."

William and Juan helped pull them aboard the boat and prepared a hot cacao chocolate drink to refresh them.

"Yes, we found an amazing clue. We found a colorful cave drawing of our former King Fire Is Born, surrounded by animals and insects. We think this must have something to do with his connection to the land. The illustration showed him surrounded by an owl, a dove, an eagle, a frog, and a butterfly," Pedro added.

"Interesting! Maybe each of those animals represent something significant to him or to the Maya. For example, an owl could mean wisdom. What do you think?"

"Very good observation, Juan," agreed Julia.

"Possibly the dove represents peace, and the eagle stands for power and freedom. Any ideas about what the frog and butterfly may signify?"

William piped in. "Well, I love frogs because they are so versatile; they thrive in water, land, *and* sand. A frog's life begins as a tadpole living in the water with gills for breathing; as it matures it transforms, its tail falls off, the frog develops legs, and it grows lungs to breathe air; then it moves onto land. Frogs thrive as well in harsh climates by burying themselves in sand and mud to hibernate through a cold winter. They live half of their life in water and the other half on land and even if something like bad weather happens, they survive by going into a very deep sleep."

"Great observation, William. Maybe to the Mayans frogs represent the duality of living in two places, like heaven and earth or Xilbalba and Earth. Frogs evolved to successfully handle bad situations like harsh weather; maybe the Mayans respected the hardiness of this amphibian," Julia surmised.

Pedro spoke again. "The butterfly could have to do with transformation and play. Since it begins life as a caterpillar, then finds itself being wrapped into a cocoon, and then breaks free to become a beautiful, playful butterfly."

"Very interesting!" Juan interjected, nodding thoughtfully. "Do you think the message could be that change is always occurring and to have faith even when we don't understand why something is happening?"

Pedro smiled and replied, "Little brother, you are wise beyond your years!"

Juan blushed and stood a little taller, the compliment from his adored older brother making him feel really good.

Cool Cat began listing animals in Spanish. "*Lechusa*...owl; *paloma*...dove; *águila*...eagle; *rana*...frog;*perro*...dog;*mono*...monkey;*mariposa*...butterfly." He smiled and continued, "*Los cambios siempre estan aconteciendo*...change is always occurring. *Tengan esperanza aun cuando nosotros no entendamos que cosas estan pasando*...Have faith even when we don't understand why something is happening."

They all sipped the refreshing hot cacao, imagining what they would find next. Pedro restarted the boat, pulled up the anchor, and sped off to Half Moon Cay Island.

SACRED UNDERWORLD

As they approached the island, the sandy shore seemed to glow brilliantly. The beaches shimmered as if they were covered with gems. Beautiful seashells and strange round and oblong green, lilac, and blue speckled rocks sparkled in the sand.

As they pulled the boat onto the shore, Juan exclaimed, "Wow! Half Moon Cay, one of the most ancient and magical places on earth!"

"This island was a sacred holy site for royalty only. And this is where the Mayan king, Fire Is Born, supposedly built a temple to worship the long nosed Rain God, Chac. Many sacred incense ceremonies and offerings to summon rain were held here. I sure hope we find this temple! Legend says when Fire Is Born died the island was cursed by the neighboring king of Calakmul. The curse was so powerful that no one dared step foot on this island. We may be the first to set foot on its banks since that curse!"

William fidgeted nervously. "I hope it's safe for us to be here. What are these colored stones? Where are the emeralds, rubies, and pearls that are supposed to be covering the beaches?"

Julia laughed and hugged William. "William, we're safe. I'm here with you. And this must be jade!"

Suddenly, loud noises of yelling, screeching, and screaming permeated the air, filling their ears with its discordant sounds.

William screamed. "What's making those horrible noises?"

Pedro put his hand on William's shoulder to calm him. "That must be the infamous Howler Monkeys. They're the loudest animals in the world, and they hide in the trees and are rarely seen."

"They sound really scary. Do they attack or bite?"

"Yes, they can bite," Pedro responded, "but their bark is louder than their bite. They are very small monkeys that developed this sound to scare away their enemies. They won't hurt us as long as we don't hurt them."

Unbeknownst to them, on the other side of the island Dr. Diamond and Crow had landed their own boat. They also marveled at the beautiful seashells and stones scattered on the beach. Dr. Diamond picked up a handful of the green, lilac, and blue stones and sifted them through his fingers. Jade. "So they've found the ancient island of Half Moon Cay where King Fire Is Born was said to have built a great temple to Chac almost two thousand years ago. I wonder if this is where the magical green jade mask was hidden so many years ago! According to the ancient *stelae* or carved hieroglyphics in stone, a magical jade mask was buried in an underground cave temple," Dr. Diamond told Crow, "and the person who finds this jade mask will rule this land, once again bringing peace, prosperity, and plentiful harvest to its people."

Crow seemed to smirk at hearing the words *peace*, *prosperity*, and *plentiful*—as if nice words and images offended his sensibilities. "How do we know this story is true?"

Dr. Diamond drew a breath, trying to seem patient. "Many years ago records were kept chronicling all the times of war, peace, prosperity, and the prophecies that were made and the legends told." He paused, then continued, "We must find out what those meddlesome kids are up to. Go find out and report back to me."

Crow squawked and flew away to gather information for Dr. Diamond.

Loria the butterfly whispered to Julia. "We have not-so-friendly visitors we must be aware of."

Julia thanked Loria, pictured the power color purple surrounding her to give her insight, and stayed alert as she had been cautioned to do.

When she rejoined the group she said, "Let's see what secrets we shall uncover!" They all sat and analyzed the map on the back of the medallion: Three fingers, seven Ceiba trees in descending size, and a big, deep X marking what might be the legendary treasure.

Pedro had a suggestion. "Maybe the X is carved so deeply because it is deep in the earth, like inside a cave?"

Julia paused to think about the suggestion. "Yes, great thinking! If we can find the three fingers and the seven trees that might lead us to an underground cave or possibly a temple!"

"Let's all stay together," Pedro said. "I have a strange feeling we're being watched—and not just by curious monkeys."

Julia agreed, "I have the exact same feeling. It's creeping me out."

Juan and William shuddered. "Great idea, staying together. Glad we thought of it!"

The howling monkeys continued to scream. Crow landed on a tree nearby and watched them from behind a profusion of leaves camouflaged by the wet, dark-brown branches.

As they walked through the jungle, they spotted red parrots, reddish egrets, blue crowned motmots and a peculiar black crow that Julia noticed was very focused on her group. Why was it following their every move and not flying away? It was as if the bird were spying on them. Just then, with Pedro leading the way to head right around the island, they passed the first finger, then the second finger. Soon, the seven descending ceiba trees came into view.

Julia exclaimed, "Look! The ceiba trees! The Maya believed that the universe had three levels: the heavens, the earth, and the underworld. They believed the sacred ceiba tree was in the center, its branches touching the heavens and its roots descending into the underworld. They called these trees the Tree of Life."

The kids scurried over to the trees and noticed beautiful, rare black orchids growing at the trunk bases. There was also a peculiar leafy plant all around the trees. At the furthest of the seven ceiba trees, there was a large thicket of bushes and bramble.

Juan examined the leafy plant. "This is the same peculiar green leafy plant that grows next to Rao's doghouse."

Pedro bent down to look. "This plant is called chaya and has incredible healing properties. Our people have used it for many thousands of years to stay healthy and vibrant. It is full of vitamins, protein, calcium, and iron. We eat it almost every day, Juan! And for those of you who don't know what the Spanish is, it's also called—"

He was interrupted by Cool Cat who cried out, "Spinach!"

Pedro giggled and chucked the cat under its chin. "Yes, spinach!"

Juan, picking up on the silly mood, exclaimed, "It's no wonder I'm so big and strong and Rao is such a healthy and tough dog!"

Pedro laughed, "Here! Let's cut through this bram-ble. Maybe we will find the actún, or ancient cave!"

All the kids and even Rao dug maniacally at the brambles and bushes to make a hole big enough to crawl into. Rao did not wait for them and jumped right through the hole and disappeared.

Crow flew back to Dr. Diamond and reported that the children had found the cave. Dr. Diamond realized this must be the cave Wally Leon had spoken about all those many years ago. He thought about the Mayans' use of caves serving as portals for the world of the humans to the underworld of the gods or to Xilbalba, the place of fear and darkness. The Maya believed that deities like the rain and earth gods, evil gods of death and disease, and even their own human ancestors resided in these caves. They performed many sacred rituals, including offering the scent of heaven by burning copal, the bark of a tree that smells very sweet. They also stored sacred items and ancestral skeletons in caves for safekeeping.

The Maya also believed that if anyone dared to venture into Xilbalba, he or she would face a battery of tests: the first test being the river of scorpions; the second, the river of blood; and last, the river of pus. They believed also that a supreme god, Hunab Ku, had created all of the rivers, trees, and animals.

Dr. Diamond was mulling over all these facts as he and Crow hurriedly their way back to the thicket. He wondered if this was where Wally Leon had hidden the prized trillion ruby. . . .

Suddenly six bats flew out from the bramble. Pedro started. "I found a large opening; it looks like a cave with a staircase, and it has pools of water as well!" Pedro lit two large torches that were at the opening of the *cenote*. He handed one to Julia. "Now follow me closely!" Unity, the dove, guarded the entrance.

The staircase opened wider as it descended, and the torchlight revealed colorful drawings lining the walls. Terraced platforms on the sides of the steps stored vessels that could have been for water or juice. The colorful drawings were of city life, children playing, women gathering water at the well, men hunting for game.

As they descended, the drawings became more graphic: large temples with altars of Chac-mool, a reclining human figure that held the human heart sacrifices being offered to the gods; rubber ball games called pok-ta-pok that were similar to soccer only the losing team was put to death. This ball game was a public reenactment of warfare, and the captives were forced to play the royal victors with a predetermined victor; in other words, the games were fixed. The losing team lost their heads. The Maya believed human sacrifice appeased the gods and kept them from harming the rest of the group; they sacrificed young women and children in order to receive more rain for bountiful crops.

William exclaimed, "Oh no! Are we in trouble? Are the Maya still performing human sacrifices with children?"

Pedro chuckled. "No, don't worry. Almost 600 years ago, the Mayan civilization and their old ways ceased to exist. No one is sure of the reason for their downfall; some say they were victims of their own success. The Maya were masters of astronomy, math, and time; they began using the 365-day solar calendar in 100 BCE—way before the Europeans in the 1580s ACE. They were skilled farmers, and knew all about irrigation, but their population grew quickly; soon there was not enough food to sustain all of the people. Many legends passed down mentioned great droughts that led to more and more sacrifices to appease the gods. This led to more conflict; and many believe that ultimately a large part of their destruction was due to their warring nature."

Juan looked at William. "This reminds me of those bullies—Tarke, Clark, and Marque—always trying to fight and push others around because they think it will get them what they want—whatever that is."

"Another reason to promote peace-filled lives," said William. "Fighting just leads to the destruction of civilizations."

The two boys nodded and said simultaneously, "Agreed!"

"Bullying and fighting have to stop!" added Juan.

"Do you think if the Maya had worked together toward common goals for the welfare of all the people that they would still be thriving today?"

Pedro nodded, musing. "Very interesting observation, Julia. It's very difficult to say. Maybe the Mayan attitude of violence combined with scarcity of land, crops, and water resources created more fear among the people. The Toltec people, once a part of the Mayan civilization, parted ways with the Maya and moved north to create a more spiritual and peaceful community. They did not believe in human sacrifice and believed there was abundance enough for everyone."

"Did they thrive because they shared the crops, didn't fight, and helped each other?" William asked.

"Yes, they were peaceful, and thus powerful and prosperous," answered Pedro.

"Wow, maybe this is something we can learn from and share with other people. Perhaps being generous, helpful, and peaceful will lead to our civilization's continued existence and our living in harmony." Julia had always been interested in ancient civilizations and history, but it had not occurred to her until that point that the ancients might have something to teach her today.

The children caught up to the excited and bouncy Rao and continued to explore further, deeper and deeper into the cave.

THE AWAKENING

The cave suddenly opened into a large expansive room nearly the size of a small cathedral. It seemed to be formed from a translucent green material that glistened.

"Oh my goodness, what a glorious room!" Julia exclaimed. "I've never seen anything so magnificent. I am sure this is jade!"

William and Juan's mouths dropped open.

Cool Cat was at a loss for words even though a few did come out. "*Espléndido!*...Splendid! *Magnífico!*...Magnificent! *Bello!*...Beautiful! *Fantastico!*...Fantastic!"

In the room's center rested an elaborate carved stone altar with images of Chac, the rain god, surrounded by a natural spring water stream. They wandered past large vessels, machetes, carved serpents, eagles, coyotes, cats, and most notably Balam the Jaguar, lord of the jungle. The room seemed to glow with overflowing treasures.

Julia noticed a smaller room off the main corridor; as she slowly walked toward the opening, she felt an ominous shiver travel from her head to her toes.

Loria whispered to her, "Yes, Julia, follow your instincts; you'll be fine if you do. It's time for you to discover the truth of who you really are, the powers you really have."

Julia walked into the smaller room. The entire room was completely mirrored, making it seem much larger than it was. Julia became a little dizzy, looking at her own reflection all around her. On the right side of the room, a small chest rested on a platform that jutted from the wall.

She walked to the chest, sat down, and began to open it. Just then she noticed a set of dark eyes peering at her through the mirror. A little nervous and scared, she said, "Who are you?"

The eyes peered back. "It is you! We are blessed; you have finally arrived! Open the chest! Your search is over, though your quest has just begun."

Julia wanted to ask more of the voice and the eyes, but her curiosity was too much. Slowly she opened

the chest. Inside was the exquisitely carved ruby trillion. She gasped. The missing piece for the center of the pendant! It was triangular in shape. Someone had painstakingly carved a landscape of animals, insects, and plants all over the ruby. The ruby and its workmanship were breathtaking.

The eyes whispered again. "This ruby trillion was given to you by your grandfather, Wally Leon."

Julia was surprised, yet relieved. She couldn't help but wonder how the eyes knew about her pendant. Come to think of it, how did the eyes know her grandfather?

Then it struck her: Her grandfather must have been

here! She slowly reached for the ruby and held her pendant in her palm. The ruby fit perfectly into her circle of Ps pendant. She immediately felt as though a light was coursing right through her body. She was filled with an amazing sense of peace, strength, and a tremendous feeling of love for all humankind. She felt as though she were as light as a feather; there was a ringing sensation in her body, an acute feeling of connectedness with all that surrounded her.

She slowly stood up and a voice proclaimed, "You are Julia, The Generosity Genie. From this day forward, you will give your sacred and joyful vow to follow the secret order of the Gen G. You will honorably share our sacred Five Ps of Peace, Play, Passion, Prosperity, and Power with everyone you meet. Now go and spread our word so you can help many generations to experience life as it is meant to be."

Julia felt honored. "Yes, I respectfully and joyfully vow to follow the secret order of The Generosity Genie: to share the sacred Five Ps of Peace, Play, Passion, Prosperity, and Power with all."

The ruby glowed brightly in her pendant medallion. Peace radiated in the room and she felt consumed with love.

Loria fluttered joyfully around the room, knowing

Julia's life would be forever altered. Loria grew in size, and mysteriously, a new color—red—appeared on her purple, blue, and yellow wings.

William asked, "Where did Julia go?"

Just then, Julia joyfully and confidently walked back into the main room. She felt kind of dazed. She also felt very different. Then she actually heard Unity outside the cave, whispering a warning that unwelcome visitors had descended the stairs.

William ran to Julia. "Where have you been?"

With a smile, she quietly responded, "Taking care of a long-awaited discovery." She pointed to her pendant.

"You found the missing piece?" William exclaimed.

Julia grinned hugely. "Yes, I found the missing piece—and so much more!"

William gazed at her curiously; he had never seen her look quite so beautiful and strong...something seemed different. He would have to ask what it really was later, for more pressing issues were at hand. He pointed. "Julia, look, there on the wall: the drawing of Fire Is Born with the goggles around his eyes—he looks like he's half owl."

Sure enough, Fire Is Born was rendered on the wall with the owl, dove, eagle, frog, and butterfly situated around him just like they had been in the cave at the Blue Hole. He remembered that the owl represented wisdom, the dove stood for peace, the eagle signified power, the frog meant prosperity, and the butterfly was all about play.

Juan walked over and placed his two fingers in Fire Is Born's owl eyes as if he knew just what was required. As he did, the whole wall mysteriously started to open. They all stood and stared, transfixed. The opening revealed a room that was light green in color—all carved in jade! In the center of the room they could see a large jade sarcophagus with Fire Is Born's face carved on the top.

They entered and walked over to the jade sarcophagus, an ancient stone coffin. They tried to open it, but the lid was extremely heavy.

Juan said, "Let's all push from this side and open it." They pushed and pushed and the lid reluctantly slid open. To their amazement, they had uncovered the wrapped and preserved body of Fire Is Born himself! There he lay, the famous green jade mask, as beautiful as the legend had declared, covering his face. Cinnabar covered his body. They had found the famous king and the long lost mask!

While staring at the body, Julia noticed that Juan's

facial features strongly resembled Fire Is Born's. "Juan, you and Fire Is Born look so similar you could be related."

Pedro nodded slowly in agreement. "Juan, you've found the special opening in the wall; you also found the ancient medallion and the green jade mask. As legend would have it, whoever finds this mask will once again rule this land and bring peace and prosperity to its people. You are this person!"

Juan stood a little straighter and said, "Wow, what an honor! But I'm not old enough nor do I have any experience in ruling the land or bringing peace to our people. How can I possibly be the one?"

"It's been a thousand years, and you are the one who found this mask; it is your destiny. Only you will know for sure." Then Pedro added, "Ancient wisdom says to look inside you and ask the question; the answer will be revealed. Do you feel you are the chosen one? Do you feel it in your heart?"

Juan thought about it, trying to listen carefully to his body. He remembered how he had recently learned to stand up for himself against the bullies. He paced back and forth, finally exclaiming, "Yes, I do feel it! I *am* the one who will return peace to our lands."

William jumped up and down, so excited for his

new friend Juan to be the new ruler of the Maya lands. They were all so excited they did not notice another figure in their presence.

Dr. Diamond and Crow listened and watched this unveiling. Dr. Diamond then stormed into the jade room. He grabbed the mask from Juan and proclaimed, "It is mine now! I am the chosen ruler, and I will rule this land! You will never be seen again!" Crow swooped around the room, screeching and laughing. Dr. Diamond noticed Julia's pendant and ripped it from her neck, "This is mine now, too! Your beloved Grandfather Wally no longer wins—I do!"

Pedro, Juan, William were all surprised! William blurted out, "What do we do now?"

Julia heard Unity and Loria whisper, "Summon the animals; they will come to protect and help you." In her mind, Julia began to call forth the snakes, iguanas, howler monkeys, fire ants, scorpions ladybugs, scarab beetles, dragonflies, toucans, macaws, and cockroaches that she knew inhabited the island. "Come help us, come help us," she pleaded silently.

Dr. Diamond motioned to Crow and he and the bird tied everyone together, back to back. "You will meet your doom here in this ancient cave!"

Juan whispered sadly, "The legend was wrong.

Our people will *not* be saved and peace will *not* be brought to our lands. We'll all die here, and nobody will know what happened to us."

Pedro tried to comfort Juan even though his little brother was tied to his back. "Have some faith. Things you cannot yet see may be unfolding."

Slowly but surely, insects came out from the cracks in the walls, boa constrictors appeared from the holes, rodents large and small swarmed into the cave. As the squirrels gnawed upon the ropes, freeing Pedro, Julia, William, and Juan, the macaws, alligators and rats blocked Dr. J. D. Diamond and Crow from escaping. Dr. Diamond looked both surprised and scared, and he did not move a muscle.

"Thank you, animals and insects, you saved us! We're free! Now let's get the green jade mask and my pendant back!" Julia said.

Juan nodded. "Yes, now I'm really ready to help my people and bring peace and prosperity back to our lands."

Cool Cat, happy to be saved, purred loudly. "*Vamos a salir de aqui*...let's get out of here!"

The animals held Dr. J. D. Diamond and Crow prisoner. Julia grabbed the green jade mask, handed it to Juan, then took her pendant and placed it around her neck. She proudly proclaimed, "Evil never wins. Now, go! Get lost! I never want to see the two of you again!"

Dr. Diamond and Crow slinked out of the cave and ran for their lives back to their boat. The animals followed them to make sure they left. Dr. Diamond looked at Crow and said, "This time we were defeated by the enemy, but we'll be back!" They revved up their motor and sped off in a speedboat.

Julia, William, and Pedro jumped for joy. "We found the green jade mask! And we've also found our new leader!"

"Juan, when we get back to the mainland, I am going to proudly introduce you to the tribal council. They will be honored and happy to recognize your new position among our people! It's a wonderful time to come into power, because the ancient Maya believed the universe was created four times and that the present cycle would come to an end on December 21, 2012 ACE. The change was to bring a joyous time of discovery and inner adventure as well. It is a time we all look forward to celebrating."

William shook Juan's hand. "I'm proud to call you my friend. It's been an unforgettable and unimaginable time together!"

Juan bowed his head. "I feel like I've grown so much

in this short time with you. I've gained confidence to stand up for myself and stop bullying. I'm committed to helping lead our people to create a prosperous and peace-filled life. I feel powerful and strong—but totally peaceful in my heart!"

Julia, now also known as Gen G, the Generosity Genie reveled, "We've had our first amazing adventure together, and the first of many as we travel around these lands, exploring ancient civilizations. I'm so grateful to all of our friends!

"Thank you for your generous and giving ways. You helped rescue me from the *cenote*. We worked together to build Rao's doghouse. We stood up against the bullies and Dr. Diamond and that awful Crow. We used power gems and colors to help us feel confident, courageous, and protected. Now we will promote peace with passion, take each step with joy and love, and know that our journey from beginning to end is what matters most. Help us spread PEACE, PLAY, PASSION, PROSPERITY, and POWER to all. Ready? Fire! Aim! Love and blessings to everyone!"

Unity, Loria, and Cool Cat smiled at each other. Then Cool Cat went back to licking a fresh salmon filet, muttering in between purrful chews, "*Paz...* peace; *jugar...*play; *pasión...*passion; *prosperidad...* prosperity; *poder...*power. *Hasta luego! Muchas buenas bendiciones!* Until later! Many good blessings! *Los queremos.* We love you!"

In the end, it was not such a hard lesson to share. Julia and William knew that bullying behavior could only exist when the heart was not part of the equation between the two sides. They knew that by teaching each child who he or she really is would help the child find their own humanity, their own special purpose in life. Promoting peace-filled lives was a fun adventure that everyone could share in.

"I love the song of the mockingbird,
Bird of four hundred voices,
I love the color of the jadestone,
And the enervating perfume of flowers,
But more than all I love my
brother: man."

—Poems of Nezahualcoyotl,
No blood sacrifices, First temple, 15th century

Power Gems & Colors Chart:

Clear: Diamond, Quartz ~ Faith ~ Abundance ~ Energy

Purple: Amethyst, Lepidolite, Sugilite ~ Protection ~ Wisdom ~ Insight

Red: Ruby, Garnet, Carnelian, Red Jasper ~ Courage ~ Strength ~ Passion ~ Power

Pink: Pink Quartz, Pink Tourmaline, Kunzite ~ Self Love ~ Expression of Love for Others, Life

Orange: Sapphire, Garnet ~ Creativity ~ Play

Yellow: Citrine, Topaz, Sapphire ~ Clarity ~ Confidence

Green: Emerald, Peridot, Jade, Malachite ~ Healing

Blue: Sapphire, Aquamarine, Blue Lace Agate, Turquoise, Celestite, Azurite ~ Peace ~ Communication ~ Prosperity

Brown: Quartz, Tigers Eye, Dravite ~ Manifesting

Black: Obsidian, Tourmaline, Hematite ~ Grounding
~Protection

Gold: Pyrite ~ Focus ~ Calm